THE
CARROT SEED

THE
CARROT SEED

Story by Ruth Krauss

Pictures by Crockett Johnson

HarperCollins*Publishers*

A little boy planted
a carrot seed.

His mother said, "I'm afraid it won't come up."

His father said, "I'm afraid
it won't come up."

And his big brother said,

"It won't come up."

Every day the little boy pulled up the weeds around the seed and sprinkled the ground with water.

But nothing came up.

And nothing came up.

Everyone kept saying it wouldn't come up.

But he still pulled up the weeds around it every day and sprinkled the ground with water.

And then, one day,

a carrot came up

just as the little boy

had known it would.

HAWTHORN OPTION SCHOOL
810 Aspen Drive
Vernon Hills, IL 60061